VEGETABLES

by Robin Nelson

first step nonfiction

Lerner Publications Company · Minneapolis

We need to eat many
different foods to stay **healthy**.

We need to eat foods in
the **vegetable** group.

Vegetables are parts of plants.

Vegetables give us **vitamins**
and **minerals**.

Vegetables help our bodies heal.

Vegetables help our eyes
stay healthy.

We need three **servings** of
vegetables each day.

We can eat lettuce.

We can eat corn.

We can eat carrots.

We can eat peas.

We can eat broccoli.

We can eat yams.

We can eat green beans.

We can eat peppers.

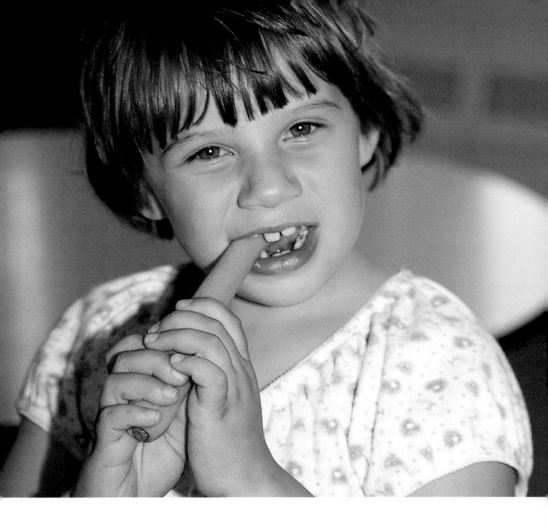

Vegetables keep me healthy.

Fats, Oils, and Sweets
Use Sparingly

Milk, Yogurt, and Cheese Group
2-3 Servings

Meat, Poultry, Fish, Dry Beans, Eggs, and Nuts Group
2-3 Servings

Vegetable Group
3-5 Servings

Fruit Group
2-4 Servings

Bread, Cereal, Rice, and Pasta Group
6-11 Servings

Vegetable Group

The food pyramid shows us how many servings of different foods we should eat every day. The vegetable group is on the second level of the food pyramid. You need 3–5 servings of vegetables every day. You could eat a cup of lettuce or ½ of a cup of broccoli. You could drink ¾ of a cup of vegetable juice. Vegetables give you vitamins to help you see. Eating vegetables helps our bodies to heal cuts and bruises.

Vegetable Facts

 Vegetables come from plants. The part you eat could be the stem, flower, leaf, seed, or root of the plant.

 June 17 is National Eat Your Vegetables Day.

 Most pea pods contain an average of 8 peas.

Carrots contain a lot of vitamin A. Vitamin A helps your eyes to see, especially at night.

 Darker green lettuce leaves are better for you than lighter green leaves.

 Spinach was the first frozen vegetable to be sold.

Glossary

 healthy – not sick

 minerals – parts of food that keep your blood, bones, and teeth healthy

 servings – amounts of food

 vegetable – a part of a plant that you can eat

 vitamins – parts of food that keep your body healthy

Index

The photographs in this book have been reproduced through the courtesy of: © Todd Strand/ Independent Picture Service, front cover, pp. 3, 5, 6, 7, 8, 9, 11, 12, 13, 15, 16, 17, 22 (top, second from top, middle, bottom). © PhotoDisc/Royalty-Free, p. 2. © USDA, pp. 4, 10, 22 (second from bottom); © Steve Foley & Rena Dehler/Independent Picture Service, p. 14.

Lerner Publications Company
A division of Lerner Publishing Group
241 First Avenue North
Minneapolis, MN 55401 USA

Website address: www.lernerbooks.com

Library of Congress Cataloging-in-Publication Data

Nelson, Robin, 1971–
        Vegetables / by Robin Nelson.
            p.   cm. — (First step nonfiction)
        Includes index.
        Summary: An introduction to different vegetables and the part they play in a healthy diet.
        ISBN: 0–8225–4626–4 (lib. bdg. : alk. paper)
        1. Vegetables—Juvenile literature. [1. Vegetables. 2. Nutrition.] I. Title. II. Series.
TX391 .N45 2003
641.3'5—dc21   2002013615

Manufactured in the United States of America
1 2 3 4 5 6 – JR – 08 07 06 05 04 03

U.S. $3.95
CAN. $6.95

Food Groups

DAIRY

FATS, OILS, AND SWEETS

FRUITS

GRAINS

MEATS AND PROTEINS

VEGETABLES

First Step Nonfiction

ISBN 0-8225-4627-2

50395

9 780822 546276

LERNER CLASSROOM

MEATS AND PROTEINS

by Robin Nelson

first step nonfiction